W9-AKS-666

The Mystery of the Butterfly Garden

Elspeth Campbell Murphy
Illustrated by Joe Nordstrom

BETHANY HOUSE PUBLISHERS
MINNEAPOLIS, MINNESOTA 55438

The Mystery of the Butterfly Garden
Copyright © 1999
Elspeth Campbell Murphy

Cover and story illustrations by Joe Nordstrom

Scripture quotations are from the *International Children's Bible, New Century Version,* copyright © 1986, 1988 by Word Publishing, Dallas, Texas 75039. Used by permission.

Published by Bethany House Publishers
A Ministry of Bethany Fellowship International
11400 Hampshire Avenue South
Minneapolis, Minnesota 55438
www.bethanyhouse.com

Printed in the United States of America by
Bethany Press International, Minneapolis, Minnesota 55438

Library of Congress Cataloging-in-Publication Data

CIP data applied for

ISBN 0–7642–2131–0   CIP

The Mystery of the Butterfly Garden

THREE COUSINS DETECTIVE CLUB®

ELSPETH CAMPBELL MURPHY has been a familiar name in Christian publishing for nearly twenty years, with more than one hundred books to her credit and sales approaching six million worldwide. She is the author of the bestselling series *David and I Talk to God* and *The Kids From Apple Street Church*, as well as the 1990 Gold Medallion winner *Do You See Me, God?*, and two books of prayer meditations for teachers, *Chalkdust* and *Recess*. A graduate of Trinity College and Moody Bible Institute, Elspeth and her husband, Mike, make their home in Chicago, where she writes full time.

Contents

"Search for [wisdom] as you would for silver. Hunt for it like hidden treasure."
Proverbs 2:4

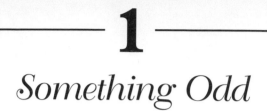

Something Odd

"*H*old still," muttered Timothy Dawson. "How do you expect me to paint your picture if you're fluttering all over the place?"

Obediently the butterfly perched on a flower and spread his wings.

"Thank you," said Timothy.

It was a monarch butterfly, Timothy's favorite kind. He was able to get down a little splotch of orange with black trim on the canvas before the butterfly flitted off again. Only a little splotch of orange and black paint. But it looked exactly like a monarch butterfly.

"Wow, Tim!" said Timothy's cousin Sarah-Jane Cooper, who was visiting. "That is so cool."

"EX-cellent!" agreed Timothy's other cousin Titus McKay.

Timothy sat back and looked at his painting.

It was a picture of a little butterfly garden. All the flowers in the garden had been chosen because they were the kind that especially attracted butterflies. Timothy already had some little yellow and white butterflies in his picture. And now the monarch. It was perfect. Except . . .

"I don't know," said Timothy. "There's something odd. . . ."

Timothy could almost *see* his cousins' ears perk up at the idea of something odd.

The three cousins had a detective club, and there was nothing they liked better than hearing about a mystery—unless it was *solving* a mystery.

"What do you mean? What's odd about it?" asked Titus.

All Timothy could do was shrug. "I don't know," he said. "Something just is."

Titus and Sarah-Jane frowned thoughtfully as they studied the painting along with Timothy.

"I give up," said Titus at last. "I don't see a thing odd about it at all."

"Me, neither," said Sarah-Jane. "It's a *wonderful* picture. And I bet it wins first prize."

The nature center was holding an art contest as part of a butterfly festival. The rules said that the paintings had to have something to do with butterflies. But they could be either real or imaginary butterflies. It was up to the artist.

Timothy thought butterflies were so naturally fabulous that he didn't have to make them any fancier. So he had decided to do a realistic painting. And he had gotten permission to paint the butterfly garden at his church.

Timothy had always been good at art—ever since he picked up his first crayon. But this past summer he had taken special art classes and worked very, very hard at it. He didn't want to get his hopes up about winning first prize, but who knew? The picture looked pretty neat-O—if he did say so himself.

"Lookin' good," said Titus, echoing Timothy's thoughts.

"Yep," said Timothy. "The monarch is the 'finishing touch.' This time of year you sometimes see a lot of them flying by. They go to Mexico for the winter."

"*Winter?*" said Sarah-Jane. "It's still only September. It's still nice and warm."

"I know," said Timothy. "But somehow the monarchs know when it's time to get going. And somehow they know where to go. No one really knows how they do it. Anyway, I *love* monarch butterflies. My first painting of the butterfly garden turned out really nice. It had little yellow and white butterflies in it, too. But I like this one better because it has a monarch in it."

"*First* painting?" asked Titus. "You mean you painted two pictures of the same thing? How come?"

"And what happened to the other painting?" added Sarah-Jane.

"Well," said Timothy, "that's kind of an interesting story."

2

An Interesting Story

*A*t the idea of an interesting story, Timothy
could tell his cousins' ears perked up even
more. He hoped they wouldn't be disap-
pointed. It *was* an interesting story. A mystery,
even. It's just that he didn't know yet how it
would turn out.

"Well, see," he began, "there's this pair of
silver candlesticks that belong to the church.
Very fancy. Very old. And, I guess, really val-
uable. Then one day not too long ago, they just
up and disappeared."

Titus and Sarah-Jane blinked at him.

"You mean they were stolen?" asked Titus.

Timothy shrugged. "I guess so. One day
they were there the same as usual, and the next
morning they were gone. I guess someone just

walked off with them. But no one ever expected anything like this to happen. I mean, the candlesticks were there for years. And people come into the church all the time just to sit quietly. Or they can come out to the butterfly garden if they want. So who knows? This might mean the church will have to be kept locked up all the time. Even though I know Pastor Parry doesn't want to have to do that. It's too bad when someone ruins things for everybody else."

The cousins were quiet for a moment, just thinking about all this.

Then Sarah-Jane said, "But what do the missing candlesticks have to do with your painting, Tim?"

"Well," Timothy replied, "Pastor Parry was so nice about how much he liked my picture that I gave it to him to make him feel better about the candlesticks."

"That was a nice thing to do," said Titus.

"I guess so," said Timothy. "I don't know how much it helped. But he seemed really happy about it. He even hung it up in the hallway by the church office."

"So that's what happened to the first painting," said Sarah-Jane. "Can we go see it?"

"Sure," said Timothy.

"Did you think there was something odd about that picture, too?" asked Titus.

"No," said Timothy with some surprise. "Now that you mention it—no, I didn't."

3

Trudy-the-Terrible

*T*imothy left the painting on the easel to dry and led his cousins into the church by the back door. Then suddenly he stopped in the hallway and looked quickly around. Titus and Sarah-Jane ran right into him.

"Shh!" whispered Timothy. "I forgot to warn you! Watch out for Trudy!"

"Cute name!" exclaimed Sarah-Jane.

"Yes," said Timothy impatiently. Sarah-Jane was always getting sidetracked by girl stuff. "Sometimes she even spells it with an *i*. With a little flower or a heart over it. But that's not the point! Trudy is no sweetheart, believe me. I call her Trudy-the-Terrible."

"Yes, but who is she?" asked Titus.

"She's Mrs. Parry's niece," said Timothy.

"She's staying with them for a couple of weeks. Her mother sent her to help out while the church secretary is away. But I heard Pastor Parry tell someone that Trudy and her mother just needed a break from each other. You know what teenage girls are like."

Titus and Sarah-Jane glanced at each other and smiled. Timothy knew it was no secret that he and teenage girls did not get along. At all.

"Hello, punk," said a voice behind him. "Who let you in?"

Timothy jumped but tried not to show it. "Who wants to know?" he replied.

Before the girl could answer, Titus smiled sweetly and said, "You must be Trudy. Tim has told us so much about you."

"Yeah, I'll bet," muttered Trudy. "Who are you?"

"We're Tim's cousins," said Sarah-Jane quickly. "I'm Sarah-Jane Cooper, and this is Titus McKay."

Trudy barely nodded at Titus. But she beamed at Sarah-Jane.

"I *love* your hair!" she declared. "Is that your natural color?"

Timothy groaned.

Sarah-Jane burst out laughing. "Of course it is! My mother would never let me dye my hair."

"*Tell* me about it!" exclaimed Trudy, rolling her eyes. "Mothers can be *so* un*reas*onable! I mean, why else would I be here, working my fingers to the bone?"

"Well, don't let us keep you," said Timothy, super politely. "I'm sure you have a ton of work to do."

"We just came in to see Tim's painting,"

explained Sarah-Jane all in a rush as Trudy scowled at Timothy. "He just finished a new one. It's out on the easel. But Tim thinks there's something odd about it. So we want to see the first one, too."

Timothy expected Trudy to say, "There's something odd about Timothy." But she didn't. She just blinked as if she couldn't quite take in everything Sarah-Jane was saying. Then she pointed vaguely down the hall to where the painting was hanging and hurried away.

4

The First Picture

*T*itus and Sarah-Jane followed Timothy down the hallway to the spot where his first picture was hanging on the wall.

It was the perfect spot for it, because it hung next to a window where you could look out over the lawn and see the real butterfly garden.

But Timothy shook his head and said, "I must be going crazy, because now *this* painting looks odd to me."

Timothy knew that his cousins were too polite to call him crazy, but they were looking at him a little funny.

"OK, OK," said Timothy with a laugh. "I guess there's nothing wrong with either painting. Maybe I'm just nervous about the contest or something."

"That must be it," said Sarah-Jane. "Because this painting looks fine to me."

"Me, too," said Titus.

"Me, too," said Pastor Parry, coming out of his office. "It's a lovely painting, Timothy. You should be very proud of it. I'm delighted to have it—though I'm sorry you had to go to all the work of painting a new one."

"Oh, it's no trouble at all," said Timothy. "If you don't mind, I think I'll leave it out there to dry a little bit. We'll get it when we come back from lunch."

(Timothy didn't have to introduce his cousins because they had visited before. But everyone said, "Nice to see you again.")

"No problem about the painting," said Pastor Parry. "I'll tell Mrs. Parry to keep Buddy Boy away from the garden so that he doesn't accidentally knock over the painting."

Titus had just opened his mouth to say "Who's Buddy Boy?" when a big brown dog came trotting out of the office.

Buddy Boy went straight to Titus. Animals

always did. He had a special way with them—especially dogs.

"Oh, you're a *good* boy, aren't you?" said Titus. "Yes, you are. You're a good, good boy."

Buddy Boy just ate this up.

"He's a great dog!" Titus said to Pastor Parry. "How long have you had him?"

"We just got him, actually," Pastor Parry replied. "Since the burglary, we thought it might not be a bad idea to have a dog around the church grounds at night. And, of course, our house is right next door to the church. So we went to the Humane Society and adopted Buddy Boy. He wouldn't hurt a fly, but if anyone came prowling around, Buddy Boy would bark his head off."

Sarah-Jane said, "We were really sorry to hear about the burglary. Was anything taken besides the candlesticks?"

She was asking to be polite, but also because detectives are always curious.

Pastor Parry shook his head with a puzzled smile. "My wife says some dish towels are missing from the church kitchen. But we think that must be some kind of coincidence."

Titus said, "I've heard of stuff getting stolen from churches. Not dish towels. But money. And the fancy stuff you sometimes see in churches. Like—I've heard of thieves actually cutting out stained-glass windows.

"And then there was this time some burglars took some carved antique chairs from the front of the church. Later on, a church member saw the chairs at a flea market. So he gave the guy some money to hold the chairs and said he was coming back with a van. But actually he came back with the police.

"So the police caught the crooks, and the church got their chairs back."

Pastor Parry said, "It's great the way that worked out! But I'm afraid our candlesticks could be anywhere by now. I doubt if we'll ever see them again."

The cousins didn't know what to say to that. They liked it when things worked out, but they knew sometimes they just didn't.

5

Good Dog

"Woof!" said Buddy Boy, as if to assure everyone that he wouldn't let any burglaries happen again.

Sarah-Jane said, "Maybe a burglar wouldn't even try to break in if he saw such a big dog. After all, the burglar wouldn't know that Buddy Boy is just a big old teddy bear. That's what you are, aren't you, Buddy Boy? Just a big old teddy bear."

Buddy Boy pulled his attention away from Titus for a minute to get fussed over by Sarah-Jane.

"Yes, that's what he is, all right," agreed Pastor Parry. "Although Trudy's rather afraid of him. He's a little clumsy, but he doesn't mean any harm."

"That's like my dog," said Titus. "He doesn't mean any harm, either. We have a Yorkshire terrier named Gubbio. And he's a very sweet dog. But Yorkies love to dig. That's just something they do. My mom has these big flower pots on the balcony. So Gubbio dug up the flowers."

"What??" said a sharp voice behind them. "What did you say? Who's been digging up flowers? What flowers?"

Honestly! Timothy thought as he jumped again and tried not to show it. *Why does Trudy always have to sneak up on people? And what does she care, anyway?*

"My dog," explained Titus. "I was telling how he dug up my mother's flowers."

"Oh," said Trudy, sounding suddenly bored. "I don't like dogs."

"How can anyone not like dogs?!" demanded Titus.

"Well," said Sarah-Jane brightly, before a fight could break out. "We really should be getting home for lunch. We'll come back later for the new painting."

"Oh, that reminds me," said Pastor Parry. "We're going to get this one framed. It's so nice for people to be able to look at the picture and then look out the window at the actual garden."

His painting framed! Timothy was thrilled to hear that. He gave a little laugh. "Then I guess there really is nothing wrong with it."

"Of course not!" said Pastor Parry. "It's perfect just the way it is." He gave a friendly wave and went back into his study with Buddy Boy.

On the way out, Timothy happened to glance back.

What he saw surprised him.

Trudy was looking closely at his painting. Really studying it—the way people did in art museums.

Timothy left before Trudy could notice him. But he thought that, of all the odd things he had seen that day, that was the oddest.

6

Really Weird

"*T*hat's funny," said Timothy when they came back from lunch to pick up the painting.

"Funny ha-ha or funny weird?" asked Titus.

"Funny *weird*!" exclaimed Timothy. Funny—really, really, *really*—weird."

"What's funny weird?" asked Sarah-Jane.

"The butterfly is gone!" said Timothy.

His cousins stared at him blankly for a moment.

Then Titus, sounding very puzzled, said, "You mean the butterfly you were painting? The monarch? Why did you think he would still be here? Don't butterflies just come and go a lot?"

"No, no, no," said Timothy. "I mean—yes,

butterflies *do* come and go a lot. But I'm not talking about the *real* butterfly. I'm talking about the *painted* butterfly. The butterfly in the painting. It's gone! Look!"

Titus and Sarah-Jane looked where Timothy was pointing.

His beautiful painting of the butterfly garden stood on its little easel exactly where they had left it.

But the monarch butterfly—the finishing touch on Timothy's picture—was gone.

7

The Missing Monarch

*T*imothy, Titus, and Sarah-Jane stood staring at the painting in disbelief.

"How could this happen?" asked Titus at last. "Is it possible someone came along and painted over it?"

"Not unless he brought his own paints," said Sarah-Jane. "Tim took his home at lunch, remember?"

"Right," agreed Titus. "And people usually don't carry paints around with them. But even if someone *did* have his own paints, why in the world would he paint over someone else's picture? It doesn't make sense."

Timothy was only half-listening to his cousins' conversation. "The flowers are wrong, too," he muttered. "I wouldn't have painted them like that. I was trying so hard to paint exactly what I saw."

"What do you mean?" asked Sarah-Jane. "What's wrong with the flowers?"

Timothy pointed to the front of the garden. "Do you see those little clumps of marigolds? The gold ones are on the right, and the dark red ones are on the left. But in the *picture*, the *gold* ones are on the left and the *dark red* ones are on the right. I don't understand how I got it backward. And I *really* don't understand what happened to the monarch. You guys *did* see me paint it in, right?"

Titus and Sarah-Jane nodded vigorously.

"Then where is it now?" asked Timothy. "It didn't just fly away, that's for sure. So what happened? I left my painting out to dry, and someone came along and switched the colors of the marigolds and painted out the monarch?!"

Timothy reached out to touch his painting. Carefully. He didn't want to smudge it. It would still be wet—especially if someone had painted over parts of it.

The painting was bone dry.

"OK," said Timothy. "That settles it. I

have officially lost my mind. This is not the painting I was working on this morning. It can't be."

"But—but what are you saying, Tim?" asked Titus. "That this is your *other* painting? The *first* one? Then what happened to the *new* one? The *second* painting?"

Without a word, all three cousins turned and looked at the church.

There was something they had to check out.

8

An Amazing Discovery

"*T*his is crazy," muttered Timothy as he led his cousins back into the church. "How can my first painting be outside in the garden when it's supposed to be inside, hanging on the wall?"

"It *was* inside," said Sarah-Jane. "We saw it ourselves when we came inside before we went home for lunch."

"And it looks like it's still there," added Titus. "Or at least *something* is." He pointed down the hall to where a picture hung on the wall next to the window.

The cousins went to take a closer look.

And that's when things got even crazier.

The painting on the wall had little yellow and white butterflies in its garden—just like the first picture.

But it also had a monarch—just like the second picture.

It was also still wet.

The three cousins looked at one another in amazement.

Titus said, "This is the picture you just finished, isn't it? *This* is the second picture."

"It sure is," said Timothy.

"Then what's it doing in here when it should be out in the garden?" asked Sarah-Jane. "What happened? Did someone switch the paintings?"

"Sure looks that way," said Timothy grimly. He pointed to a couple of small smudges at the edge of the canvas. "Whoever moved it was careful, but not careful enough."

"But why move the painting at all?" asked Titus. "It doesn't make sense. Pastor Parry was very happy with the first painting. He said so. But even if he liked the second painting better, he would never have switched the paintings without asking you, would he?"

Timothy shook his head firmly. "No, Pastor Parry would never have messed with the paintings. I'm sure of that."

He glanced at the door to the study. A sign said, *Back this evening.* So Pastor Parry was gone. And there didn't seem to be anyone else around.

"Then who?" asked Sarah-Jane. "Who switched the paintings? And *why*?"

"Maybe it was someone's idea of a dumb joke," suggested Titus.

Again Timothy shook his head. But he was less certain of himself this time. "I think there's some sort of reason. I just don't know what it is. But I'll tell you what I *do* know. Remember when I was working on this painting,

I said there was something odd about it—but I just couldn't put my finger on it?"

Titus and Sarah-Jane nodded.

"Well," said Timothy, "now I know what it is."

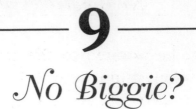

9

No Biggie?

*T*imothy took a deep breath as his cousins waited for him to explain himself.

The three cousins had rules for their detective club. And one of the rules said that if one cousin needed to explain something, the other two had to be quiet and listen and try to follow what that cousin was saying.

It wasn't always easy to get your thoughts together. But the rule was that the explaining cousin had to try hard to be understood.

It wasn't always easy to *listen* to someone who was trying to get his thoughts together. But the listening cousins had to try hard to understand.

With one hand, Timothy pointed to the painting of the butterfly garden. With the

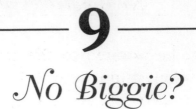

other hand, he pointed to the real butterfly garden that they could see out the window.

"See?" he said. "This painting and the garden *match*. The marigolds are in the proper order. The gold ones are on the right, and the dark red ones are on the left. When I was working on this painting, part of my brain was telling me that it was odd just because it was different from the first painting."

"So what you're saying," began Sarah-Jane slowly, "is that there's actually *nothing* odd about this painting. The second one. The only odd thing about it is that it doesn't match the first painting. And the first painting is *really* the odd one because it doesn't match the garden."

"Exactly!" said Timothy with relief. Then he added, sounding sad and puzzled at the same time, "I just don't know how I could have made a mistake like that on the first painting."

"Everybody makes mistakes," said Titus. "And this one is 'no biggie.' That's what my mom tells me when she thinks I'm being too hard on myself. No biggie. You fixed it on the second painting, after all."

Timothy smiled. He knew Titus was trying to cheer him up. But the whole thing still bothered him. "I guess it's no big deal," he agreed. "It's just that I don't understand how it happened. I was trying so hard to paint *exactly* what I saw."

Neither Sarah-Jane nor Titus had an answer for that. They both knew Timothy was super careful about his artwork.

"So what do we do now?" asked Titus.

"Switch the paintings back," said Timothy firmly. "I want to enter the one with the monarch in the nature center contest. Pastor Parry was happy with the first painting, so we'll just put it back where it was."

Very, very carefully (because it was still wet), Timothy carried the second painting out to the garden.

Titus and Sarah-Jane picked up the first painting and propped it against a rock. Timothy carefully placed the second painting back on the easel.

Then the three cousins stood back and looked at the two paintings side by side. It was a puzzle all right.

They carried the first painting back inside and hung it up beside the window in its proper place.

They were just on their way out when they ran into Trudy.

Sarah-Jane asked her nicely if she happened to know anything about the paintings getting switched.

Since it was Sarah-Jane who asked, Trudy managed not to be too snotty when she said she had no idea what they were talking about.

"Well," said Sarah-Jane as Trudy hurried away. "It doesn't hurt to ask, I guess."

"Right," said Titus. "And I'd be more inclined to believe her if she didn't have paint on her sleeve."

10

A Smudge of Paint

"*Trudy?*" Sarah-Jane said to Titus as they stepped outside. "You think *Trudy* switched the paintings? Why would she do a thing like that?"

Titus shrugged. "I don't know. Because she's a mean person?"

"Be serious!" Sarah-Jane demanded.

"OK," said Titus. "Trudy is a *seriously* mean person."

Sarah-Jane sighed and rolled her eyes. "OK, I'll admit that Trudy is not the nicest person in the world. But she doesn't seem like the type to play jokes—even really dumb ones. What do you think, Tim?"

"Actually, I agree with both of you," said Timothy. "I agree with S-J that switching paintings doesn't seem like the type of thing Trudy would do for a joke. And I agree with Ti that Trudy is mean person. So—if she was going to play a trick on me, I think it would be even meaner than switching paintings. I mean, why not hide both paintings where I would never find them? Why not *really* mess up the wet paint instead of just leaving a couple of little smudges?"

"Then how did she get paint on her sleeve?" asked Titus.

"That I don't know," replied Timothy. "Maybe she just accidentally brushed up against the painting when she was walking down the hall."

"Which means," said Titus, "that someone *else* switched the paintings. Any idea who that might be?"

"Nope," sighed Timothy. "I don't have any idea *who* or *why*."

The cousins were quiet, just thinking about this. Mysteries could be really frustrating sometimes!

But they couldn't think of anything else to do except to pick up the painting and the easel and to go home and forget about the whole thing.

Except that they knew they wouldn't be able to forget about it. That was the really frustrating part.

It was then that Timothy took one long, hard last look at the garden.

"You guys!" he said. "Come look at this!"

11

Mysterious Marigolds

*T*imothy pointed right at the clumps of marigolds.

"Don't they look funny to you?" he asked.

"Funny ha-ha or funny weird?" asked Titus.

"Oh, let's not start *that* again!" cried Sarah-Jane.

"Funny weird," said Timothy.

"What's funny weird?" asked Titus.

"The ground around the marigolds is kind of churned up," said Timothy. "Like maybe someone was digging there or something. It's kind of hard to tell. You have to look closely to see it."

Titus and Sarah-Jane looked closely at the spot where Timothy was pointing. And, sure

enough, the ground around the marigolds *did* look a little more churned up than the ground around the other flowers in the butterfly garden.

"See?" cried Timothy happily. "That proves it! There's nothing wrong with my first painting. There's something wrong with the garden!"

"Huh?" said Titus and Sarah-Jane together.

"Well, isn't it obvious?" said Timothy a little impatiently. "Someone's been *switching the marigolds!*"

"Huh?" said Titus and Sarah-Jane together.

"Someone's been switching the marigolds!" Timothy repeated. "When I painted my first picture, I *did* paint exactly what I saw. The gold marigolds were on the left, and the dark red ones were on the right. My painting matched the garden the way it was. But then someone came along and dug up the marigolds and *switched them*! So when I painted my second picture, I painted exactly what I saw again. But the garden was different. So that's why my second painting was different. That's why the two paintings don't match. This clears everything up!"

"Huh?" said Titus and Sarah-Jane together.

The detective cousins had a rule. It said that the listening cousins couldn't make fun of the talking cousin no matter how crazy something sounded.

So Titus and Sarah-Jane didn't call him crazy. But Timothy could tell they thought he had been out in the hot sun too long.

"Tim," said Titus carefully, "why would anybody *do* that? Dig up marigolds, I mean. And switch them around?"

Timothy thought about this. Maybe he *had* gotten a little carried away. "I don't know," he said at last. "I just got so excited when I saw that the ground was a little bit churned up. I thought I had found a logical explanation for why my two pictures are different. But I guess it's not logical to think someone would go around switching marigolds. I was letting my imagination run away with me."

Sarah-Jane, whose imagination was always running away with her, said in the most matter-of-fact way, "I know how we can find out."

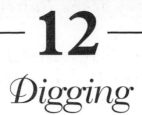

12

Digging

*T*imothy and Titus stared at her.

"Well, think about it," said Sarah-Jane. "Gardens don't just happen. People *plan* them. Even gardens like this one that are supposed to look a little wild are all planned out ahead of time.

"I know a lot of people who have gardens. And they draw diagrams of how the garden is supposed to look before they even start planting. It's sort of like making a little map of where to put the flowers. That's how it is here. See how the tall flowers are in the back and the medium flowers are in the middle and the little flowers are at the edge? That's so you can see them all.

"Someone planned the whole thing. Now

all we have to do is talk to that person and ask how the garden is supposed to look."

"A diagram!" said Timothy. "I never thought of that! Mrs. Parry planted the garden. Let's go see if she's home."

They raced across the yard to the pastor's house next door.

Mrs. Parry was home, and so was Buddy Boy, who greeted them like long-lost friends.

"I guess you guys can come rob us anytime," said Mrs. Parry with a laugh. "Buddy Boy would even hold the door open for you."

"But not for a real burglar," said Sarah-Jane.

"Let's hope not!" said Mrs. Parry. "Now, what can I do for you?"

It took a while—quite a while—to explain about the mixed-up paintings and the mixed-up marigolds. But Mrs. Parry listened carefully. She was known for being a good listener and for being well organized. It took no time at all for her to find her diagram of the butterfly garden where she had filed it away for next year.

Soon the four of them (and Buddy Boy,

too, of course!) were hurrying back across the yard to the garden.

"Well, for goodness' sake!" cried Mrs. Parry. "You kids are right! The marigolds *are* in the wrong place. How in the world did *that* happen? I'm usually so careful about things like that. I knew exactly how I wanted the garden to look."

"And I knew exactly how my painting of the garden should look," said Timothy, turning to stare meaningfully at his cousins.

Titus grinned at him. "Hey, what can I tell you, Tim? When you're right, you're right."

Mrs. Parry said, "I hope you kids don't think I'm crazy, but I'd like to switch the marigolds back to the way they're supposed to be. I think they look better that way."

"I agree," said Timothy. Then he added politely, "We don't think you're the least bit crazy, Mrs. Parry. We'll help you move the flowers if you like."

"That would be nice," she replied. "I'll get something for us to dig with."

She was back soon with gardening tools. Carefully they dug up the two clumps of marigolds, being sure not to damage the roots.

Mrs. Parry was just about to replant the flowers when Timothy said, "Wait! There's something down there!"

13

The Bundle

What Timothy saw was a little scrap of white plastic.

Quickly he scooped away some more dirt. An ordinary white plastic trash bag.

"What in the world—?" said Mrs. Parry.

"Who buries garbage in a flower garden?" asked Sarah-Jane.

"Maybe it's not garbage," said Titus. "You could put just about anything in a trash bag."

"We'll soon find out," said Timothy.

Carefully he hauled the bag out of the hole—

"It's heavy!"

—and laid it on the grass.

The cousins looked to Mrs. Parry, who opened the bag and gave a little cry of surprise.

"What? What is it?" asked the three cousins together. They crowded closer to get a better look.

"It's the missing dish towels from the church kitchen!" exclaimed Mrs. Parry in a voice that said she couldn't believe her eyes.

"But—how can that be?" asked Timothy. "Dish towels aren't heavy."

"No," said Mrs. Parry grimly. "But these dish towels are wrapped around something. Three guesses what that might be."

The cousins didn't need three guesses.

They got it right the first time.

Mrs. Parry unwrapped the dish towels.

The missing silver candlesticks glinted in the sun.

Mrs. Parry sat back on her heels and looked at the cousins. "Well! I must say I don't know what to make of this. Do you?"

The cousins slowly shook their heads.

"Tell you what," said Mrs. Parry briskly. "Let's get these marigolds replanted. In the right order, of course!"

They all laughed.

"And then I'll call Pastor Parry and let him know the candlesticks have been found. After that—well, I don't know what else we can do. It's a mystery to me how they got there. If you have any ideas, I'd be glad to hear them."

(Mrs. Parry knew about their detective club because the cousins had once solved another mystery at the church.)

After the flowers were replanted and Mrs. Parry had gone to make her phone call, the cousins turned to one another.

"Well?" said Sarah-Jane.

"Do we have any ideas?" said Titus.

"A few," said Timothy.

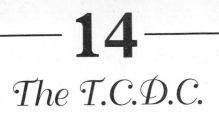

14

The T.C.D.C.

*T*imothy said, "The first thing we know is that it was not a coincidence the dish towels disappeared at the same time as the candlesticks."

"No," said Sarah-Jane. "It wasn't a coincidence. The thief used the dish towels to wrap up the candlesticks so they wouldn't get scratched. And putting them in a trash bag made the bundle waterproof. At least the thief was careful."

"The thief wouldn't get a good price for them if they were all scratched up," said Titus. "But that's what puzzles me. Why didn't the thief just take the candlesticks away and sell them? The candlesticks and the thief could have been long gone by now. It doesn't make sense to bury them close by. No sense at all."

"The thief must have been in a hurry," said Sarah-Jane. "Because he didn't put the marigolds back the way he found them. He got them mixed up."

"Also—maybe it was dark, and he couldn't see the colors well," added Timothy.

"You know," said Titus, "everyone thought the thief was just someone off the street. But this is sounding like an inside job to me. The candlesticks are wrapped in the church dish towels. Then they're buried in the church butterfly garden."

"Not to mention the paintings," agreed Sarah-Jane. "The paintings were switched between the hall and the garden. What was that all about? A thief who came in from the outside wouldn't care about the paintings, would he? And would someone from the outside even have a chance to switch them?"

Timothy said, "Well, there is one person who had paint on her sleeve. It wouldn't hurt to ask her a few questions."

Trudy was sorting papers in the church office when the cousins came in.

She was not glad to see them.

"Go away. Can't you see I'm busy?" she snarled.

"We're busy, too," said Timothy. "That's the thing about the T.C.D.C. You put us anywhere near a mystery, and we're busy, busy, busy."

Trudy frowned at him. But she couldn't help asking, "What's a 'teesy-deesy'?"

"It's letters," explained Titus. "Capital T. Capital C. Capital D. Capital C. They stand for the Three Cousins Detective Club."

"Detectives?" snorted Trudy. "*You* guys? Oh, give me a break. No offense (she said to Sarah-Jane), but what do three little kids know about anything?"

"Oh, you'd be surprised," said Timothy. "I think we'd better have a little talk."

15

A Little Talk

*T*o Timothy's surprise, Trudy didn't throw them out. *She wants to know what we know,* thought Timothy. *That's a good sign we're on the right track.* His ideas came together even as he was talking.

"OK, what do three little kids know?" he began. "Well, for one thing, we know that you stole the silver candlesticks, wrapped them in the church towels, and then put them in a trash bag.

"We know that you buried this whole bundle in the butterfly garden. But—either because you were in a hurry or because it was dark, or both—you got the clumps of marigolds in the wrong place when you put them back.

"You didn't realize what you had done until I started saying there was something odd about my paintings.

"I saw you studying my first painting. You didn't know I saw you, but I did. It wasn't that you *liked* the painting. It was that you were scared about it. You were afraid someone would notice that the painting and the garden didn't match. You were afraid someone would start wondering how the marigolds could have gotten switched. So you took my second painting—which *did* match the garden—and hung it in the hall. You hoped I would just take the first painting and go home, didn't you?"

"I wish you would go home *now*," said Trudy. "Because everything you're saying is totally ridiculous. I don't know anything about digging up flowers."

"That's not true," said Titus. "Why else would you get so freaked out when I was telling about Gubbio digging up my mom's geraniums? It was because you didn't know I was talking about my dog. You thought someone had been digging here in the butterfly garden."

"This is so boring!" said Trudy. "I don't know anything about mixed-up marigolds or mixed-up paintings. The only thing mixed up around here is you guys! I never even came near either one of your precious paintings!"

"I'd be inclined to believe you," said Titus, "if you didn't have paint on your sleeve."

Trudy gasped and twisted around to see the back of her arm.

"How about telling the truth for a change?" said Timothy.

"How do you put up with these guys?" Trudy asked Sarah-Jane.

Sarah-Jane didn't answer that. Instead, she had a question of her own. "We know *what* happened. But we don't know *why*. Why would you *do* something like that?"

Trudy sighed. "I didn't steal the candlesticks. Not really. I mean, they were still here at the church. Right?"

"Give me a break," said Timothy.

"OK, OK," said Trudy. "I took the candlesticks. It was right after I first got here. My mom never lets me have enough money. So I thought I could sell the candlesticks and buy stuff. But I knew I couldn't hide them in my room here, because my aunt might find them. I needed to put them somewhere for safekeeping. So one night when my aunt and uncle were out, I hid the candlesticks in the garden."

Sarah-Jane was shocked. "Your aunt and uncle are so nice to you! How could you do something so mean to them?"

"I know, I know," said Trudy. "I felt lousy about it."

"Then why didn't you dig the candlesticks up and put them back?" asked Titus.

"I couldn't!" cried Trudy. "Because right after I took the candlesticks, they got that dumb old dog. I couldn't sneak out to the garden because he would have barked his head off!"

"He is *not* a dumb old dog!" yelled Titus. "He's probably smarter than *you* are!"

"Oh, yeah?" snarled Trudy.

"Yeah!" snarled Titus.

"Let's change the subject," said Timothy. "So what were you going to do? Just leave the candlesticks in the garden forever?"

"No," said Trudy as if this was the dumbest question she had ever heard. "I had it all planned out. After I got home, I was going to send the church an anonymous letter, telling them where the candlesticks were. It would be like I was pretending to be the thief."

"You *were* the thief," Timothy pointed out."

"Not really," said Trudy.

"TRUDY!" exclaimed Sarah-Jane.

"OK, OK," sighed Trudy. "I guess I was the thief. So now what are you guys going to do? Tell on me, I suppose."

"No," said Timothy. "But I think you'd better tell on yourself. If your aunt and uncle don't suspect you now, they probably will soon. And it would be better if you talk to them first before they talk to you. You need to tell them you're sorry. You *are* sorry, aren't you?"

"Of course I'm sorry, you little squirt," said Trudy.

The cousins watched as Trudy headed over to the house to talk to her aunt.

"Well, pardners," said Titus in his best cowboy drawl. "I think our work is done here. It's time to be headin' fer home."

Timothy laughed. "Just let me get my painting."

The monarch was back and fluttering around the flowers.

"Don't you want to see your picture?" Timothy asked him.

As if the monarch understood every word, he came over and fluttered around the painting.

He must have really liked it, because he followed the cousins all the way home.

The End